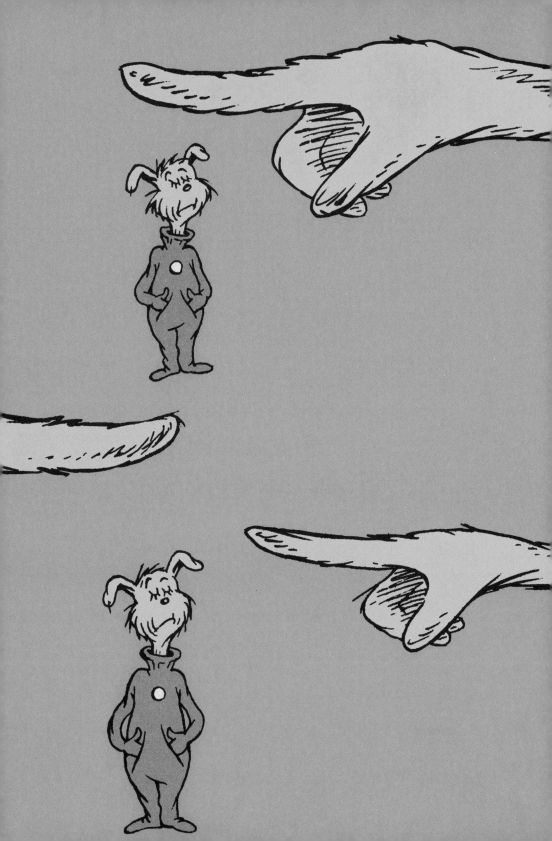

Marvin K. Mooney Will you

PLEASE GO NOW!

By Dr. Seuss

A Bright & Early Book

RANDOM HOUSE / NEW YORK

TM & copyright © by Dr. Seuss Enterprises, L.P. 1972, copyright renewed 2000.

Visit us on the Web!
www.randomhouse.com/kids
Seussville.com

Educators and librarians, for a variety of teaching tools, visit us at
www.randomhouse.com/teachers

Library of Congress Cataloging-in-Publication Data
Seuss, Dr.   Marvin K. Mooney, will you please go now! (A Bright and early book, #13)
Summary: Suggests in rhyme a number of ways for Marvin K. Mooney to travel as long as he gets going—now!
ISBN 978-0-394-82490-1 (trade) — ISBN 978-0-394-92490-8 (lib. bdg.)
[1. Stories in rhyme.   2. Fantasy.]   I. Title.   PZ8.3.S477Mar   [E]
72-1441

Printed in the United States of America
100 99 98 97 96 95 94 93 92 91 90 89 88 87 86

The
time
has come.

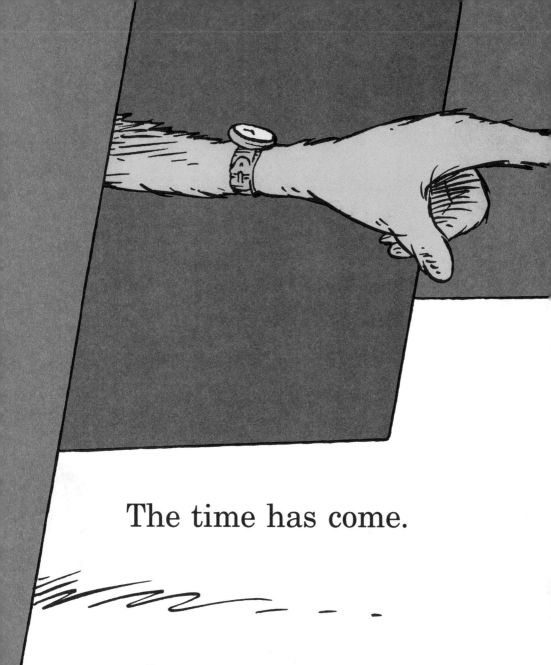

The time has come.

The time is now.

Just go.
Go.
GO!
I don't care how.

You can go by foot.

You can go
by cow.

Marvin K. Mooney,
will you
please go now!

You can go
on skates.

You can go
on skis.

You can go
in a hat.

But
please go.
Please!

I don't care.
You can go
by bike.

You can go
on a Zike-Bike
if you like.

If you like
you can go
in an old blue shoe.

Just go, go, GO!
Please do, do, DO!

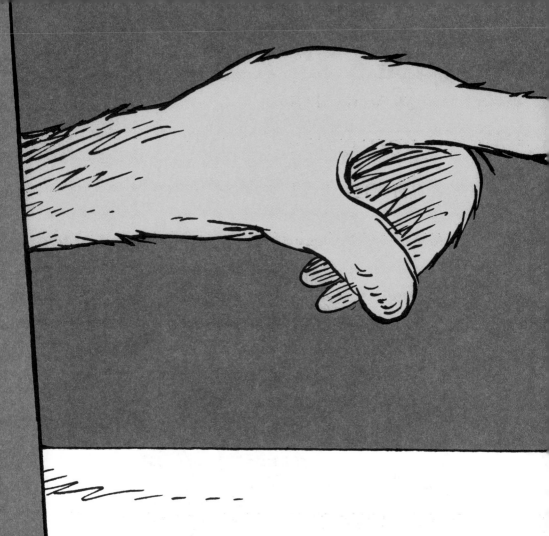

Marvin K. Mooney,
I don't care how.
Marvin K. Mooney,
will you please
GO NOW!

You can go on stilts.

You can go by fish.

You can go
in a Crunk-Car
if you wish.

If you wish
you may go
by lion's tail.

Or stamp yourself
and go by mail.

Marvin K. Mooney!
Don't you know
the time has come
to go, Go, GO!

Get on your way!
Please, Marvin K.!
You might like going
in a Zumble-Zay.

You can go
by balloon . . .

. . . or broomstick.

OR
You can go
by camel
in a
bureau drawer.

You can go by Bumble-Boat . . .

. . . or jet.

I don't care
how you go.
Just GET!

Get yourself a Ga-Zoom.
  You can go with a . . . . . .

Marvin, Marvin, Marvin!
Will you leave this room!

Marvin K. Mooney!
I don't care HOW.

Marvin K. Mooney!

Will you please

GO NOW!

I said

GO

and

GO

I meant. . . .

The time had come.
SO . . .
Marvin WENT.